A CLOSE CALL

Amanda Harvey

MACMILLAN CHILDREN'S BOOKS

to Grace and Jonah
with thanks to Carolyn and Jonathan

First published in Great Britain 1990 by
MACMILLAN CHILDREN'S BOOKS
A division of Macmillan Publishers Limited
London and Basingstoke
Associated companies throughout the world

ISBN 0-333-52388-1

Printed in Hong Kong

It was late. The Nurse was asleep, but the baby –
who had a bad cough – was awake and playing
with the Nurse's watch,

so no one noticed the time stop and the old woman creep in

and sneakily take the baby off.

A moment later the Nurse woke up; she saw her
baby was gone and ran quickly down the stairs
and out of the house,

following the old woman

until she saw her disappear through a door.

The Nurse burst in

and saw the baby on the old woman's knee.
"Give me my baby!" she cried.
"Not on your life," said the old woman,
and popped the baby in a drawer.

"I said give me my baby right now," shouted the Nurse very loudly; but the old woman just stood there, whistling and looking at her fingernails.

So the Nurse, furious now, seized a vase and
threw it at the old woman.
The vase crashed to the floor in pieces as the old
woman mumbled, "Such a pretty little baby, such
a sweet little thing. I'll give the little treasure
some syrup for its cough."

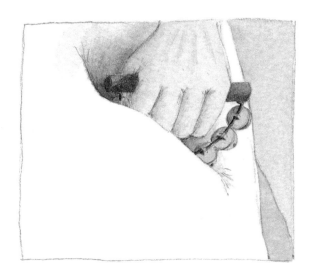

The Nurse, not knowing what else to do, took
from her pocket the baby's toy bells and beat out
a little tune:

Oats, peas, beans and barley grow,
Oats, peas, beans and barley grow,
Nor you, nor I, nor anyone knows,
How oats, peas, beans and barley grow.

To which the old woman started slowly to tap
her foot and then quite soon, forgetting herself
completely, began to dance wildly round the
floor.

And while the old woman danced ever more
wildly the Nurse ran over to the drawers.

Lifting her baby out, she ran back down the
stairs, out of the house and through the woods.

As the sun rose, the Nurse and the baby arrived
safely home

(where they lived happily ever after,
and the baby was never heard to cough again).